In Memory of Bruce and Mary Conyers
In Honor of Charles and Nell Bilbro

"So vast, without any question, is the divine
handiwork of the Almighty Creator."

- Nicholas Copernicus

Where Do They Go?

Echopus Publishing
104 Cary Place
Washington NC 27889
www.echopus.com

Published by Echopus Publishing 2008

Printed in Hong Kong

Library of Congress Control Number 2008910612

Bilbro, Michael
Where Do They Go? / by Michael Bilbro: illustrated by Michael Graham

ISBN 978-0-615-23354-3

Where Do They Go?

Written by Michael Bilbro
Illustrated by Michael Graham

Grandfather, Grandfather, where do they go?
Do they wither over water, fade and fall slow?
And Grandfather, how far do they go?
Do they get lost in the clouds, stall and linger,
or perhaps tie to another child's finger?

Do you think they come down when out of sight,
slowly deflate and get lost in the night?
I hope they blast off and go really high,
to catch the tail of a comet gone by.

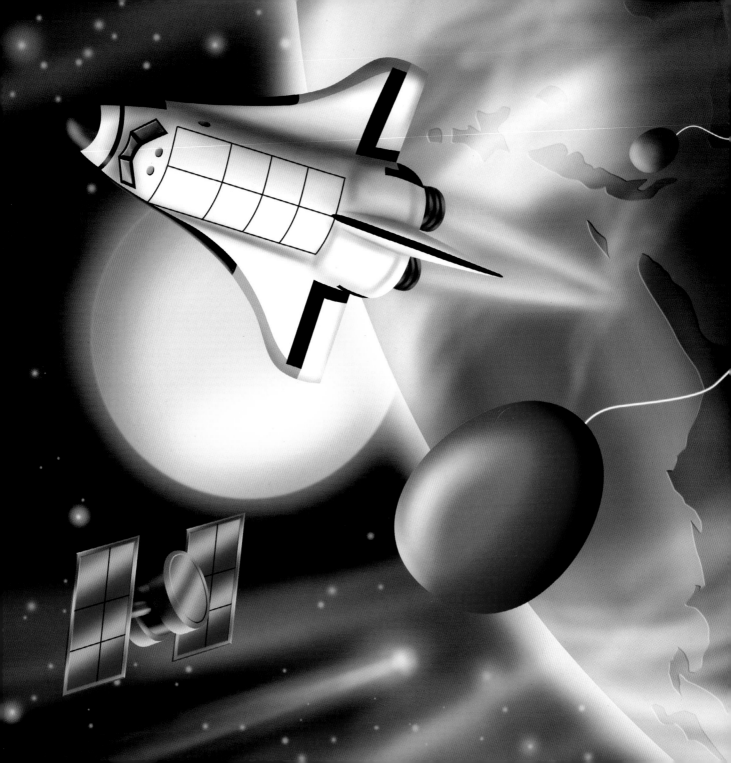

Or maybe they end by the branch of a pine.
If that is the end then I think I'll keep mine;
close to me, stringed in awe,
held tight, preventing their fall.

Sam, with all we wield it seems unfair,
to spend your life tied to a chair.
Stoic and straight, difficult to pretend,
hoping to let go, disappear and ascend.

Council Meeting
7:00 PM
Grandaddy
3 votes

So many choices, I think it depends,
on rain, snowstorms or solar winds.
Could be a Saturn ring or a Jupiter blemish,
Mercury, Venus, or a Neptune finish.

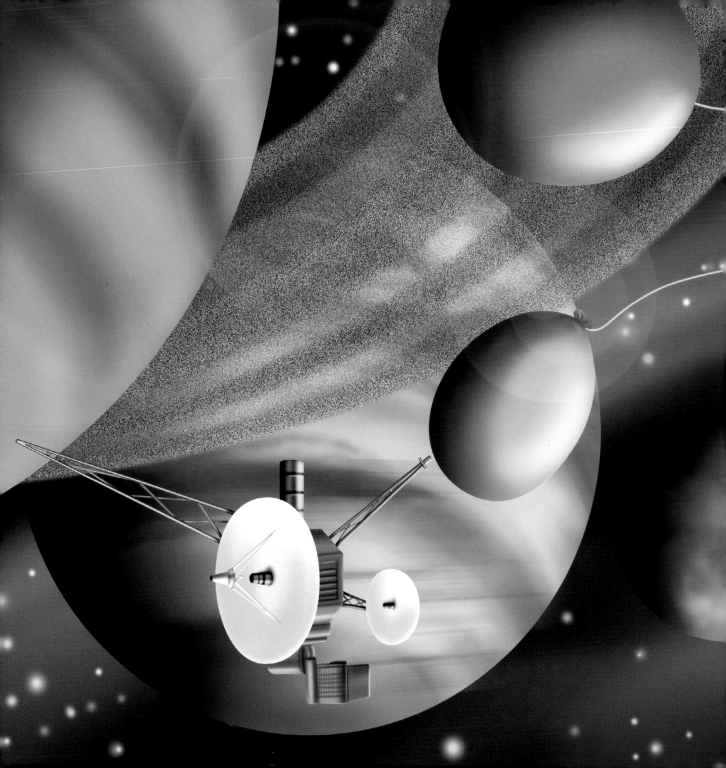

And perhaps they travel at the speed of sound,
anchored by string, far from the ground.
Through the Milky Way, skirting by Mars,
passing other systems, planets, and stars.

A straight line to a great black hole
to be caught in its grasp and never grow old.
The distance they'll go is not all that clear;
I just know it will be light years from here.

Grandfather, do you think space is the end?
Nothing beyond, not even a friend.
How sad if they fail to end up together,
sharing their colors and living forever.

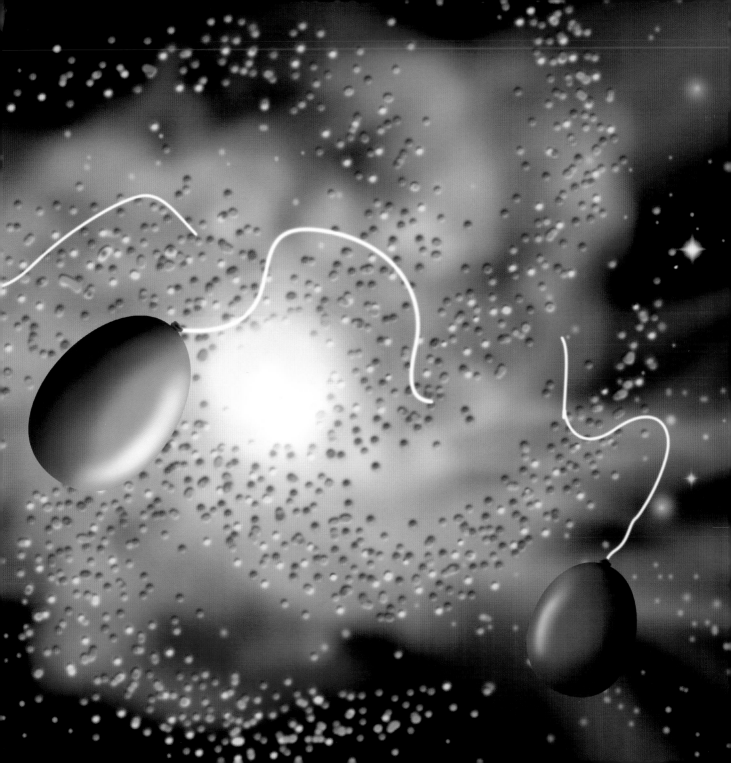

My child, the splendor of space is not the end,
and where they're going will be millions of friends.
All the galaxies and stars, a gift beyond measure,
an endless wonder, a miracle to treasure.

What a wonderful cosmos to discover and travel.
For so many unknowns, it's a lot to unravel.
I should think they journey unimaginable miles,
and end up together in a symphony of smiles.

Sam, there are billions of places to explore and see,
too much, too many for just you and me.
But not a balloon with its shell filled with air,
with no agendas, no plans, not one little care.

Grandfather, please, I just can't let go.
I want to hold on forever.... it's all that I know.
I'll not cage it by a ceiling, or block it by a wall,
I'll promise to avoid its wither, fade or fall.

Yes, you could keep it tied to a chair or a wrist,
but look at the wonder the red balloon will miss.
Unlimited discovery, boundless and free,
traversing the stars, where there's magic to see.

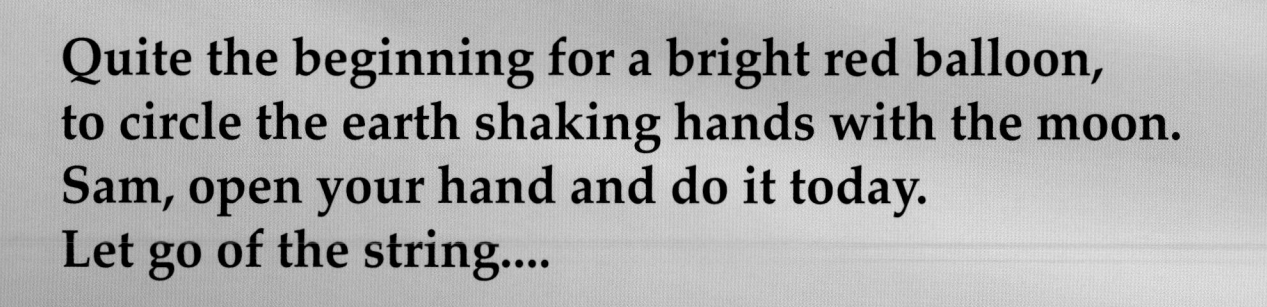

Quite the beginning for a bright red balloon,
to circle the earth shaking hands with the moon.
Sam, open your hand and do it today.
Let go of the string....